This Igloo book belongs to:

Summer Hope

igloo

Published in 2012
by Igloo Books Ltd
Cottage Farm
Sywell
NN6 0BJ
www.igloo-books.com

Copyright © 2010 Igloo Books Ltd

B044 1211
10 9 8 7 6 5 4 3 2
ISBN 978-0-85734-517-2

Illustrated by: Beverlie Manson, Diana Catchpole, Roberta Collier,
Dana Regan and Liza Woodruff
Stories retold by: Joff Brown

Printed and manufactured in China

My Treasury of Princess Stories

igloo

Contents

Snow White

Long ago, there lived a king and queen who were overjoyed when they had a beautiful, baby girl. However, soon after the child was born, the queen died. The poor king was heartbroken. He held his baby daughter and looked at her. She had lips as red as blood, hair as black as night and skin as white as snow. "I shall name you Snow White," said the king.

A few years later, the king married again. Snow White's stepmother was beautiful, but also very cruel and vain. She was secretly a witch, who had great powers. The new queen owned a magic mirror, which answered any question that was asked of it.

Each day, Snow White's stepmother always asked the mirror the same question, "Mirror, mirror, on the wall, who is the fairest of them all?" The mirror always replied with the same answer, "You, my queen are the fairest of them all."
This made the queen very happy. Secretly, she was jealous of Snow White and feared that the girl would grow to be more beautiful than herself.

One day, when Snow White had grown into a young woman, the queen asked the mirror her usual question, "Mirror, mirror, on the wall, who is the fairest of them all?"
This time, the mirror replied, "Snow White is the fairest of them all."

The queen flew into a jealous rage and decided to get rid of Snow White, once and for all. She summoned a huntsman. "Take Snow White into the forest and kill her!" she commanded. The huntsman didn't want to kill Snow White but, like everyone else in the castle, he was terrified of the wicked queen.

That night, the huntsman grabbed Snow White from her bed while she was sleeping, and took her into the dark, dangerous forest. Even though the huntsman was cowardly, he wasn't evil and he couldn't kill Snow White. Instead, he put her down safely in the middle of the forest and warned her not to return to the castle.

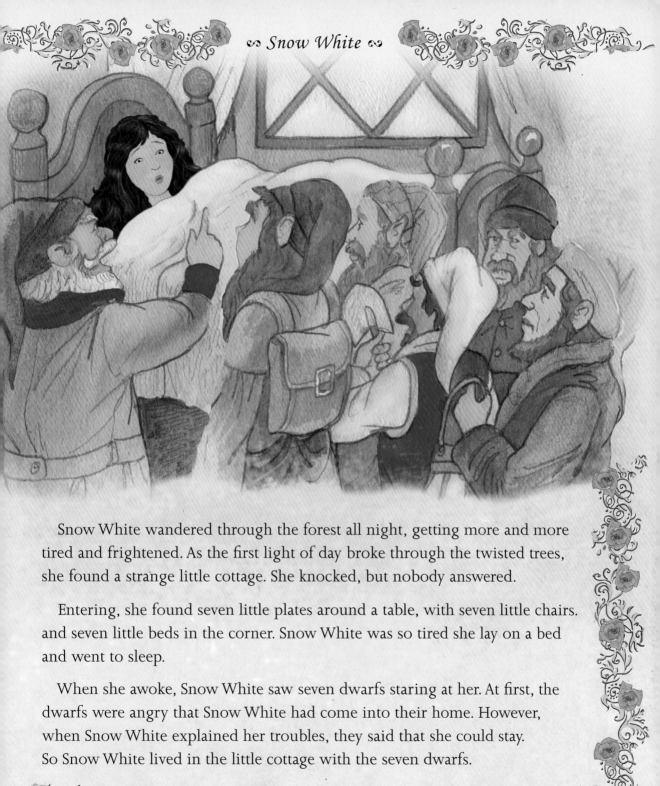

Snow White wandered through the forest all night, getting more and more tired and frightened. As the first light of day broke through the twisted trees, she found a strange little cottage. She knocked, but nobody answered.

Entering, she found seven little plates around a table, with seven little chairs. and seven little beds in the corner. Snow White was so tired she lay on a bed and went to sleep.

When she awoke, Snow White saw seven dwarfs staring at her. At first, the dwarfs were angry that Snow White had come into their home. However, when Snow White explained her troubles, they said that she could stay. So Snow White lived in the little cottage with the seven dwarfs.

Meanwhile, the evil queen asked the mirror if she was the fairest of them all. "Snow White is the fairest of them all," replied the mirror. The jealous queen was furious and asked the mirror where Snow White was. The mirror told her about the little cottage, deep in the forest.

The queen used magic to disguise herself as an old woman. The next day, when the dwarfs were working, the queen went to the cottage with an armful of pretty clothes. "Try this pretty dress on, my dear," she cackled. Snow White tried the dress on, but the queen laced it up so tightly that Snow White could not breathe. She fell to the ground and lay still. The queen fled before the dwarfs could return. She was sure that Snow White was dead.

That evening, the dwarfs returned to the cottage and found Snow White. They quickly unlaced the deadly dress and Snow White was able to breathe again. The dwarfs were relieved that no harm had come to their friend.

That night, the queen questioned the magic mirror again, only to find out that Snow White was still alive. This time, her rage was terrible to see. She enchanted an apple so that one side was full of deadly poison, but the other was safe to eat. The only thing that could break the spell was a kiss from Snow White's true love.

The next day, the queen returned to the cottage, in the magical disguise of a different old woman. "Have a bite of this tasty apple," she said. But this time, Snow White was suspicious and wouldn't touch it. "Look," said the queen, eating the side of the apple that was not poisoned. "See? It's tasty." Snow White took a bite from the poisoned side of the apple and fell down, as if dead.

This time, when the dwarfs returned, they couldn't wake Snow White. "She's dead!" they shouted. The dwarfs were very sad. They made Snow White a magnificent glass coffin and cried as they laid her in it.

Long years passed and the dwarfs guarded the coffin every day. Snow White stayed as beautiful as ever, as if she were only asleep.

One fine day, a handsome prince passed by the house and saw Snow White in the coffin. He fell in love immediately. "Who is this beautiful girl?" he asked. "I must kiss her." He opened the coffin and kissed the girl's cheek. As he did, Snow White awoke. True love's kiss had broken the curse.

The prince took Snow White to his palace and they were married straight away. Snow White asked the seven dwarfs to join them and they all lived happily ever after.

Cinderella

Once upon a time, there was a man who had a beautiful wife and a lovely daughter, called Ella. When his wife died, the man married another woman, who had two daughters of her own. They became Ella's step-sisters, but they were jealous of her and treated her like a servant. Poor Ella had to wear old, tatty clothes and do all the housework.

One day, Ella was in the kitchen, cleaning out the grate, when the two step-sisters came to see her. Ella's ragged clothes were stained and her face was covered in soot. "Look how dirty she is," crowed one sister, fluttering her fan. "She's covered with ashes and cinders."

"We should call her Cinder-Ella!" said the other sister.

From that moment on, Ella became known as Cinderella.

One day, news arrived at the house that the prince of the land was going to hold a Grand Ball at the palace. Cinderella's father made sure that his new wife, as well as Cinderella and her two step-sisters, were invited. But when the invitations came, the sisters tore up Cinderella's before she saw it.
"Too bad," they said, "the prince doesn't want you in his beautiful palace."

When the night of the ball came, Cinderella had to help her step-mother and her step-sisters dress in their fancy gowns. Then she was sent back to the kitchen, to do all the washing, while they left for the ball. When all the work was done, Cinderella sat in the cold kitchen and cried. "I'm so sad and lonely," she said, "won't anyone help me?"

The chimney of the big kitchen fireplace began to glow and sparkle, then something bright rushed out. A twinkling, fizzing light circled the kitchen and a kind-looking fairy appeared, in a shower of sparks.
"Who are you?" asked Cinderella, in surprise.
"I'm your Fairy Godmother," answered the fairy, "and you look in need of help. What can I do for you?"

Cinderella explained that she wasn't allowed to go to the Grand Ball.
"Don't worry," said the Fairy Godmother, "you shall go to the ball!"
"But how can I go dressed in these rags?" asked Cinderella.
"A little magic will fix that," said the Fairy Godmother, sweetly." She waved her wand around Cinderella's head and her rags fluttered and flapped and swished and swelled, until they had turned into the most amazing ballgown Cinderella had ever seen. It even had a pair of glass slippers to match.

"Of course, you'll need to get to the ball," added the Fairy Godmother. She waved her wand over a pumpkin and it became a magnificent, sparkly, gold coach. Cinderella was amazed and thrilled to see the wonderful coach.

Next, the Fairy Godmother searched around the garden and found a lizard and four mice. She waved her wand over them and they were transformed into a coachman and four beautiful horses. "Now you can go to the ball," said the Fairy Godmother. "But remember, all my magic stops at midnight. So make sure that you are back here before then."

When Cinderella entered the ball at the palace all eyes were upon her.
The handsome prince took one look at her and fell instantly in love.
He spent every minute of the night dancing with her.

Cinderella enjoyed herself so much she forgot to watch the big clock that
hung at one end of the ballroom. "I am falling in love with you," the prince
told Cinderella, as they danced. "Do you love me because of my fine clothes?"
asked Cinderella.
"I would love you, even if you were in rags," said the prince.

Suddenly, the clock began to strike midnight. Terrified of showing herself in her dirty rags, Cinderella broke free of the prince and ran out of the palace. In her haste, she left behind one of her glass slippers. As she was running down the palace steps, the gown turned back into rags, the coach became a pumpkin again and the rats and lizard scuttled away. Cinderella ran back to her house and nobody knew that she had ever left it.

The prince swore that he would find the owner of the slipper. "The girl whose foot fits this slipper is the girl I shall marry," he said. The prince and his pages visited every house in the land and every girl, in every house, tried on the slipper. But it was so small and dainty, nobody's foot would fit into it.

At last, the prince came to Cinderella's house. "He mustn't see you," her step-mother said, so the sisters locked Cinderella in the coal cellar to hide her from the prince. The two sisters both tried to make the shoe fit but, no matter how hard they squeezed, they couldn't squash their big feet into the tiny, delicate, glass slipper.

The prince was ready to leave when he heard knocking coming from the cellar door. Opening it, he was surprised to see a young girl dressed in rags and covered in ash and coal dust. "Let this girl try on the slipper," said the prince.

Cinderella tried the slipper on and her little foot slipped into it perfectly. The prince knew immediately that Cinderella was the girl he had danced with at the palace.

"Will you marry me and be my queen?" asked the prince.

Cinderella had never felt so happy and accepted joyfully. The prince banished the wicked step-mother and the step-sisters to a faraway land and Cinderella and the prince married without delay. Cinderella's father came to live with them in the prince's palace and all three of them lived happily ever after.

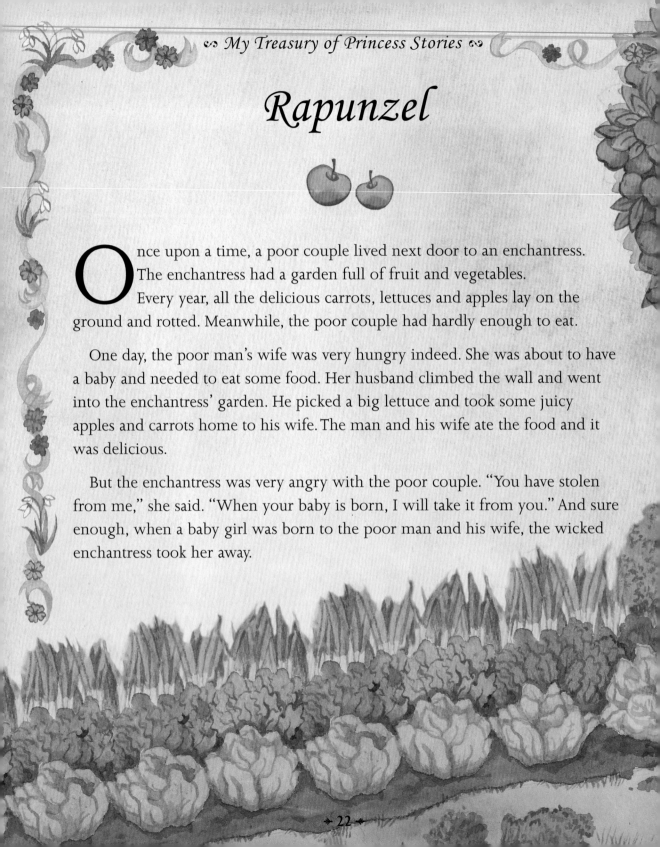

Rapunzel

Once upon a time, a poor couple lived next door to an enchantress. The enchantress had a garden full of fruit and vegetables. Every year, all the delicious carrots, lettuces and apples lay on the ground and rotted. Meanwhile, the poor couple had hardly enough to eat.

One day, the poor man's wife was very hungry indeed. She was about to have a baby and needed to eat some food. Her husband climbed the wall and went into the enchantress' garden. He picked a big lettuce and took some juicy apples and carrots home to his wife. The man and his wife ate the food and it was delicious.

But the enchantress was very angry with the poor couple. "You have stolen from me," she said. "When your baby is born, I will take it from you." And sure enough, when a baby girl was born to the poor man and his wife, the wicked enchantress took her away.

The baby was named Rapunzel and she grew into a lovely young woman, with long, golden hair. She had a beautiful singing voice and even though the enchantress hated to hear her, Rapunzel sang all day long.

One day, the enchantress took Rapunzel to a tall tower in the middle of a forest. She cast a spell on the tower, so that anyone left alone in it could never escape. "This spell cannot be undone," cackled the enchantress. "You will live here forever and I will not have to listen to you sing!"

Sometimes, the enchantress came to visit Rapunzel. She would call out, "Rapunzel, Rapunzel, let down your hair." Rapunzel would unpin her long, golden hair and lower it out of the window, so the enchantress could climb up into the tower room. The enchantress gave Rapunzel a few scraps of food and made sure that nobody had managed to enter the tower. Then she would climb back down Rapunzel's hair and scurry home.

One morning, a prince was wandering through the forest and heard Rapunzel singing. He was entranced by her beautiful voice and followed it to the tower. He saw the enchantress call out, "Rapunzel, Rapunzel, let down your hair," and then climb up the golden locks.

When the enchantress had left, the prince called out, "Rapunzel, Rapunzel, let down your hair." Rapunzel, thinking the enchantress had returned, shook her hair out the window and the prince climbed up.

Rapunzel was very surprised to see a handsome prince instead of the enchantress. Rapunzel and the prince fell in love and the prince vowed to rescue her. "I will visit you every night and bring you silk to weave into a ladder, so you can climb down the tower," the prince promised.

Night after night, the prince brought more and more silk to the tower.
It was such fine material that Rapunzel could hide it in her dress, so the
enchantress did not see it when she came to visit. But the enchantress was
clever. She saw that Rapunzel was happy and she did not know why.
She asked Rapunzel many questions, but didn't get any answers.

The enchantress became angry and grabbed Rapunzel by her dress – and the
silk came flying out in a long, billowing wave. "Wretch!" cried the enchantress.
"You have tried my patience long enough!" The enchantress grabbed her
scissors and cut off Rapunzel's long, golden hair. Then she muttered a spell and
Rapunzel found herself far from the tower, in an unknown land, with no food,
or water, and no way to reach her prince.

Meanwhile, the enchantress waited in the tower for the prince to arrive. That night, he called out softly, "Rapunzel, Rapunzel, let down your hair." The enchantress lowered Rapunzel's hair. The prince climbed up to find the furious enchantress waiting for him. "So, you're the one who tried to steal my Rapunzel, are you?" she sneered.

The prince tried to grab the enchantress, but she pushed him backwards and he toppled out of the window, pulling Rapunzel's hair down with him. The prince landed in some bushes at the foot of the tower. He looked up at the enchantress who was shaking her fist and screaming with rage. She was alone in the tower and her spell could not be undone. The evil enchantress was trapped by her own magic.

The prince set off to look for Rapunzel. He wandered far and wide, searching towns and villages along the way. The prince often heard people talk of a girl with a beautiful voice, but no matter how hard he looked, he could never find her.

After many disappointments the prince had almost given up hope when one day he heard the sweet, familiar sound of Rapunzel singing. She had found work on a farm and was singing sadly as she carried water from the well. The prince ran to Rapunzel and they embraced.

The prince took Rapunzel home to see her parents. They were overjoyed at the return of their daughter. Soon after, the prince married Rapunzel and they lived happily ever after. As for the enchantress, she was trapped in the tower for the rest of her days and never troubled anyone, ever again.

Beauty and the Beast

Once, there was a poor merchant who had three lovely daughters. The youngest daughter was the kindest and most beautiful. Her name was Belle and she loved her father dearly.

One day, when the merchant had to go on a long journey, he asked his daughters what presents they would like him to bring back. The older sisters asked for dresses and jewels, but Belle knew that her father was poor and could not afford such finery. "I only want a rose, Father," she said.

The merchant journeyed far and wide. On the way back to his village, he was caught in a tremendous storm. Seeking shelter, he found a glittering palace. Nobody seemed to be in the palace, not even the humblest servant. Every one of the huge rooms was empty. The merchant sat down to rest and saw that a table was being magically laid for him. The plates and food flew through the air, as if they were being carried by invisible hands. The surprised merchant ate a hearty meal, then decided to continue on his way.

As he was leaving the palace, he saw a rose bush and remembered his promise to Belle. The merchant reached out and picked a single, red rose. Suddenly, there was a crash of thunder and a horrible beast appeared.

The beast had a bristly, hairy head like a wild boar's, with big teeth. Its hairy arms dragged on the ground, yet it wore clothes like a man. It snorted and snuffled. "How dare you steal from me!" cried the beast, in a rage. "Is this how you repay my hospitality?"

The merchant said he was very sorry and explained that he was only picking the rose for his daughter. But the beast wouldn't be calmed. "To pay for your crime, you must send this daughter to live with me. If you do not, I will come for you and take your life!"

The merchant hurried home and told his family what had happened.
"I must go to the beast, or it will kill you," said Belle, sadly. The merchant
wouldn't let Belle leave, but that night, she climbed out of her bedroom
window and walked all the way to the palace by herself.

The beast was waiting for her. At first, Belle was terrified by the sight of such
an ugly monster, but the beast bowed and welcomed her politely.
The invisible servants prepared them a delicious meal and they ate together.
"This palace is your new home," grunted the beast. "There are many delights
for you here. And now, I have a question to ask you. Will you marry me?"

Belle was shocked. "I can't marry you. I've only just met you," she said.
The beast didn't look angry. He just nodded sadly and left.

That night, as Belle slept, she dreamed of a handsome prince. The prince seemed to be calling to her. "Save me! Please save me!" he cried.

The next day, Belle explored the palace. It was beautiful and magical. The invisible servants fetched her any food and drink she asked for. Every room was filled with beautiful dresses, gold and jewels and all manner of fine objects.

Every evening, Belle and the beast would eat together and the beast would always ask Belle the same question. "Will you marry me?"

But Belle always refused. Even though she couldn't dream of marrying such a hideous monster, she grew to love the beast. He gave her anything she asked for and in return, she was able to soften his rough manners and calm his dreadful temper.

Every night, Belle dreamt of the handsome prince. "How can I save you?" she would ask, but the prince would only say, "Don't trust appearances." There was something about the prince's eyes that reminded her of someone. But try as she might, she couldn't think who it was.

As the months passed, Belle began to miss her family. One night, she asked the beast if she could visit them for a while. "I cannot refuse you," said the beast. "But I love you so much, if you do not return soon, I shall die." The beast gave her a magic ring which transported her back home to her father and sisters.

Belle was so glad to see her family that she spent many days in their company. She almost forgot about the palace and the beast, until one night she had another dream. This time, it was the beast she saw, lying in the palace, almost dead from grief. "I have been so cruel!" cried Belle. She touched the magic ring and, in a flash, it transported her back to the palace in the blink of an eye.

Belle ran down the marble corridors and found the beast, just as he had been in her dream. He was lying on the floor, unmoving. She ran to him and cried, trying to wake him up. When her tears fell on his bristly face, he opened his eyes. "It is too late for me," he said. "I think I am going to die. Goodbye, Belle. It's a shame you didn't want to marry me."
"I will marry you, beast!" cried Belle, hugging him tightly.

The moment she said the words, Belle felt the beast begin to change. He stumbled away and turned from her and when he turned back, he was no longer a beast. In his place was the handsome prince from her dreams.

The prince smiled at her. "I was cursed by a wicked witch to be a beast," he explained. "I have lived alone for many years, too afraid to go into the outside world because of my ugliness. The only way to break the curse was to find someone pure enough of heart to marry me, even though I was so horrible to look at."

Suddenly, all the servants became visible around him and they cheered the happy couple. The prince used the magic ring to bring Belle's father and her sisters to the castle. Soon after, the prince and Belle were married and they lived happily ever after.

Sleeping Beauty

O nce upon a time, a baby girl was born to a king and queen. She looked so bright and fair, they decided to name her 'Beauty' and a great celebration was held in her honour.

Because the queen was half-fairy, she invited three of her fairy cousins to give blessings to the baby. However, she forgot to invite one distant relative – a fairy with a very bad-temper.

On the day of the blessings, the fairies gathered round the child's crib. "I give Beauty the gift of goodness and kindness," said the first fairy. "I give Beauty the gift of graceful dancing," said the second fairy.

However, before the third fairy could utter her blessing, a cold wind whirled around the crib. The angry fairy, who had not been invited, appeared. Her face was like thunder. "So, you're having a blessing without me?" she snarled, "Now this child will have my present, whether you like it or not! I curse Beauty to prick her finger on her sixteenth birthday and die!" Suddenly, the wind whirled again and the fairy vanished.

Everyone was too shocked to speak. Finally, the third fairy spoke. "I have not given my gift yet," she said in a small voice. "It is not within my power to lift the curse laid on Beauty, but I can change it a little. My gift to you, Beauty, is this – you will not die on your sixteenth birthday, but you will sleep for a hundred years, until you are awakened by true love's first kiss."

Beauty grew up to be a wonderful girl, full of the fairy gifts of kindness and grace. However, she always wondered why no sharp objects were allowed in the castle and why she was never allowed outside. She ate with a spoon, instead of a knife and fork, and she never learned to spin, or sew. Her royal parents were terrified in case Beauty should prick her finger and fall asleep.

On the day of her sixteenth birthday, Beauty was exploring the castle. In one corner of the Great Hall, she saw a little door that she had never noticed before. It led up a winding staircase, to a room in the highest tower of the castle. There, Beauty saw a woman sitting by a spinning wheel.

Beauty greeted the woman and asked what she was doing. "I'm spinning," replied the woman, who was the angry fairy in disguise. "Would you like to try spinning, my child?"

"Yes, please," said Beauty and she sat at the spinning wheel.
The fairy passed Beauty a sharp spindle, to wind the thread. Beauty took it
but, as she did, she pricked her finger. Instantly, Beauty slumped onto a dusty
old bed and fell into a deep sleep.

As soon as Beauty began to sleep, a strange thing happened in the castle.
The king and queen, on their thrones, yawned and dozed off. The court jester
slumped to the floor and the cook fell asleep in the middle of preparing dinner.
Soon, everyone in the castle had drifted off to sleep.

Around the castle moat, green tendrils began to sprout from the ground. In moments, the tendrils grew up and up and twined their way around the castle. Huge, sharp, thorns grew thickly. It was part of the third fairy's magic, to protect Beauty and the castle from harm.

When people in the outside world saw what had happened to the castle, they stayed away. Occasionally, adventures would come, seeking the riches of the sleeping king, but they were always turned back by the sharp thorns and the castle remained untouched.

One hundred years passed in silence, until a handsome prince rode by and stumbled upon the thorn-covered castle. "I must find out what is inside," said the prince. He drew his sword and cut through the thick tangle of thorns.

The prince soon found himself inside the huge castle. Everywhere he looked, there were sleeping people – the guards at the gate, the court jester snoring in the hall, even lords and ladies were lying on the great stairs. Everything was covered with cobwebs. The prince tried to wake the sleeping people, but they just murmured and went back to sleep.

As he passed through the Great Hall, the prince saw a little door standing open. It led to a tiny, winding staircase. Climbing the staircase, he found a room in the highest tower of the castle with an old, cobwebbed spinning wheel, standing in one corner. On the dusty bed, lay the most beautiful girl he had ever seen. He leaned over and gave the girl a single kiss. Beauty stirred and opened her eyes. When she saw the prince, she fell instantly in love.

The spell was broken and the silent castle began to stir. The king and queen woke up, the jester started to juggle and the cook began cooking.
The whole castle had come back to life. The prince went to the king and asked him for his daughter's hand in marriage.

In no time at all, the people of the castle had recovered from their hundred years' sleep. The prince and Beauty were married and everyone lived happily ever after.

The Fairy Queen

Once upon a time, a princess had three older sisters who loved to go to balls and parties. The princess wanted to go too, but she was too young. When her sisters were getting ready to go out, the youngest princess would go off by herself and walk around the fields and hills near the castle.

One day, the princess took a different path than usual and found herself in a wooded glade. The sun was setting and it would soon be dark. The princess knew she had to return home soon. Just as she was about to go back, she saw a glimmer nearby. It was coming from inside a ring of grass.

The princess walked towards the ring and saw pretty girls dressed in white with red caps. They were dancing hand in hand, round the ring. The princess knew this must be a fairy ring because her grandmother had often told her about them. Suddenly, the girls called to the princess, "Come and join the dance!"

As soon as the princess stepped into the ring, she saw a fine lady on a white horse appear, as if from nowhere. The lady wore a dress that was covered in pale, gleaming jewels. Her eyes seemed to glow, just like her jewels. "I am the Fairy Queen," she said. "Won't you come with us? The party is about to start."

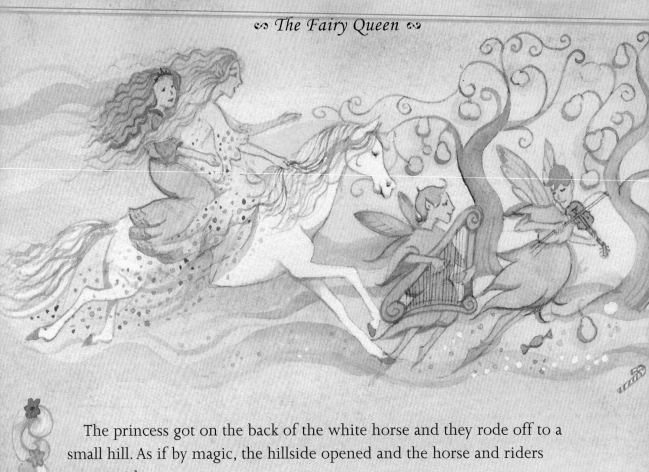

The princess got on the back of the white horse and they rode off to a small hill. As if by magic, the hillside opened and the horse and riders went inside.

The Fairy Queen took the princess into a strange and beautiful forest, where silver trees had fruit, like glass, hanging from their branches. The fruit gave off a pale light and the princess could see three fairy girls playing a harp, a flute and a violin. All around, fairy folk danced gracefully to the strange, enchanting music.

Fairy waiters moved around the guests, holding plates piled high with delicious-looking cakes and candy. The princess reached out to take a cake, but stopped suddenly. She remembered something her grandmother had once told her — anyone who tasted fairy food, or drink, would be trapped in Fairyland for a hundred years.

The princess danced until late in the night and then she said goodbye to the Fairy Queen. "Please, have a sip of some of our special apple juice before you go," said the Fairy Queen, handing the princess a golden goblet.

The princess refused to take the goblet. "No thank you, Your Majesty," she said, politely. "I have had a wonderful time. You must come and visit my palace soon."

"Thank you for your invitation," said the Fairy Queen. "We will be at your castle tomorrow night, when the clock chimes eight."

There was a sudden whirl of light and sound. The fairy kingdom disappeared and the princess found herself outside her castle, just as the sun was setting. It was as if no time had passed at all. The princess tried to tell her sisters about the Fairy Queen, but they didn't believe her. "You must have been dreaming," they said.

The next night, at eight o'clock, the princess heard the sound of hooves outside the castle. The doors opened and the Fairy Queen entered the Great Hall, followed by all the fairy folk. They started to play beautiful fairy music that was strange and magical. Soon, the people of the castle were dancing, as if bewitched.

The Fairy Queen watched with a smile, while everyone whirled gracefully around. "What pretty people," the princess heard her say. "I will take them all home with me. It will be most amusing to have them in my fairy palace."

"This is my fault," thought the princess. "If I don't do something, everyone will be spirited away to Fairyland." Then the princess had an idea. She raced down to the palace kitchens. There, she found a small piece of brittle candy and made a big hole in it, so that it resembled a ring.

The princess took the candy to the Fairy Queen. "A present for you, Your Majesty," she said, slipping the ring onto the Fairy Queen's finger. But, as soon as it had touched her skin, the ring suddenly crumbled into small candy pieces.

The Fairy Queen licked her finger. "Why, that wasn't a real ring. It was made of sugar. What a strange girl you are. But enough games," said the Fairy Queen, "you are all coming with me to Fairyland."

The Fairy Queen raised her arms to spirit everyone away, but nothing happened. "Where are my powers?" she cried. "My grandmother told me that fairy magic works both ways," said the princess. "Now that you have tasted mortal food, I'm afraid your powers are lost until you return to Fairyland."

The Fairy Queen looked furious, then amused. She nodded. "Fair is fair, Princess. We will go, but remember, the door in the hill is always open to you." Then in a flash, the fairies were all gone.

When the princess was old enough to go to the palace balls, everyone noticed that she was the finest dancer of them all. Some said it was because her sisters had taught her, but the princess knew it was because she had once danced all night with the Fairy Queen.

The Princess and the Swan

Once upon a time, a beautiful princess married the handsome prince of a high mountain kingdom. However, after the wedding ceremony, the prince said to the princess, "I cannot stay with you at night. Every evening, I must leave our palace. But every morning, I will return."
The princess was surprised and upset. "Why do you do this?" she asked.
"Please do not ask," said the prince, "I can never tell you."

The prince made the princess promise that whatever happened, she must never follow him." The danger is too great," he said. At first, the princess said she would follow the prince anywhere, but the prince begged her to promise not to. Eventually, the princess relented. "I love you," she said, "and to love is to trust."

So that night, the prince left the palace and the princess wept into her pillow. The next morning, the prince returned, just as he had promised and they spent a wonderful day together. But the next night, the prince left again, and the princess was all alone until morning.

This continued for many months, until the princess could bear it no longer. One night, she secretly watched the prince walk off in the direction of an enormous lake, which lay in the hollow between two great mountains.
"I cannot follow him, or I will break my promise," thought the princess.
"But what if he is in danger and needs my help?"

The very next night, the princess found herself creeping down the palace stairs, after the prince, to see where he went. She followed him up hills and down valleys, through woods and fields, until he arrived at a black, marshy lake. There was an island in the middle of the lake, that gleamed silver in the moonlight. On the island was a tall man, in sparkling robes. Many beautiful white swans surrounded the island. The man raised his arms and the prince seemed to shrink and grow smaller and darker. In a moment, the prince was gone and in his place was a graceful, black swan.

The swan took to the water and the man on the island shouted, "Dance, swans! Follow the prince, your leader, as you must do every night!"

At his command, the swans began to cross the lake in slow, sweeping movements, with the black swan in the lead. The man on the island laughed and sat down to watch.

The swans danced in the water, until the sun began to rise across the mountains. The princess left quickly, so as not to be seen. She saw a single tear, drop from the black swan's eye.

Back at home, the princess didn't know what to do, so she consulted a wise woman who lived near the palace. "The man on the island is a wicked enchanter," said the wise woman. "He has cursed your husband, who must dance for the enchanter every night. The only thing you can do to break the curse is to destroy the wizard's heart. But it will be hard, because he keeps the heart in a diamond and the diamond is at the very bottom of the lake."

The princess was very frightened, but she knew what she had to do. The next night, she waited until the prince had departed for the lake and she set out after him. Once the swans began their eerie dance, she knew she had to act. The princess dived into the water, to get the diamond, but the enchanter saw her and cast a magic spell that pulled her towards him.

"So, this is your wife," he said to the black swan. "Because she has broken her promise to you, your curse is doubled. You will be a swan forever!"

The princess cried in shame, but the black swan looked at her and said, "I forgive you. You loved me so much that you wanted to save me. Now, dive again, quickly."

The black swan turned to the enchanter and ran at him, pecking at him with its sharp beak and beating him with its wide wings. The enchanter cried out with rage. He turned from the swan and tried to grab the princess but, quick as a flash, she plunged into the lake and was soon out of his reach.

Holding her breath, the princess dived down and down, into the murky depths. Suddenly, she saw something glinting on the bottom of the lake.

The enchanter's heart was inside a gleaming diamond. Grabbing it, the princess swam back up, as fast as she could. She reached the surface and with all her might, the princess crushed the diamond in her hand.

There was a cracking noise and the diamond shattered. Instantly, the enchanter turned into a cloud of silver smoke that blew harmlessly away. The black swan shimmered and grew, until the prince was standing by the princess' side once more. She rushed into his arms and they held each other. When the princess let go of the prince, she saw that they were surrounded by men and women, all dressed in white.

"These were the other swans," explained the prince. "They are my loyal servants from the palace. The enchanter cursed them to stay here forever and he would have killed them all if I had not returned every night to dance with them. But now the curse is lifted and we are all free."

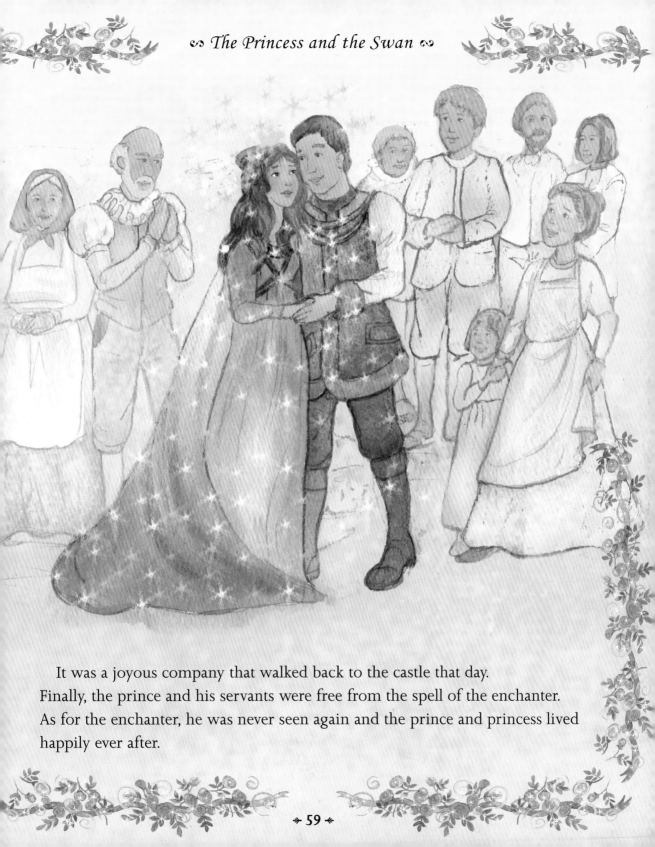

It was a joyous company that walked back to the castle that day.
Finally, the prince and his servants were free from the spell of the enchanter.
As for the enchanter, he was never seen again and the prince and princess lived
happily ever after.

The Snow Queen

Once upon a time, there was a boy named Kay and a girl named Gerda. They were best friends and loved to play together among the flowers in Gerda's garden.

One winter's day, when they were playing outside in the snow, Kay tasted a snowflake that was falling from the sky. The snowflake was cursed by dark magic and suddenly, Kay felt his heart grow cold. Instead of seeing the goodness in all that was around him, he only noticed the things that were bad and ugly.

From that day on, Kay didn't play with Gerda. Instead, he preferred to look at snowflakes with his magnifying glass. "Snowflakes are much nicer than flowers," said Kay. "Flowers are boring!"

Poor Gerda was left alone, while Kay played on his sled with all the older boys. One day, a strange, white sleigh stopped nearby. It was pulled by two beautiful, white horses and Kay tied his sled to it. To his surprise, the sleigh sped off across the snow and pulled him along for many miles.

When it stopped, Kay saw a pale lady, dressed in white fur. "I am the Snow Queen," she said. Come under my cloak to get warm." So Kay slipped under the cloak of the Snow Queen. As he did, his heart froze over. He forgot all about Gerda and the friends he had left behind.

The Snow Queen took Kay by the hand and they flew through the air. They landed in the frozen north, at the Snow Queen's ice palace, which had a great lake at the centre. The palace was a mighty fortress of snow and ice and the Snow Queen made Kay a prisoner there. He had no memory of his old life.

"I must go on a long journey," said the Snow Queen. "By the time I get back, I want you to put all the ice on my lake back together." The ice on the Snow Queen's lake had split into hundreds of pieces, like a giant jigsaw puzzle. Kay sat by the frozen lake and moved the pieces around, but the puzzle was impossible to solve.

Meanwhile, Gerda spent her days looking everywhere for Kay. She spoke to the older boys, who told Gerda that Kay had gone north with a strange sleigh. So she walked and walked, through fields and forests. Wherever Gerda went, she asked about Kay, but nobody had seen him.

After many adventures, Gerda found herself in a cold land. There was nobody to be seen, except for a herd of reindeer. As they trotted past, she called out to them, "Have you seen my friend, Kay?"

The reindeer walked past, as if they hadn't heard her, except for one old reindeer. "I have seen this boy," he said. "He was being carried on a sleigh with the Snow Queen. She traps boys and keeps them in her ice palace."

When she heard this, Gerda wept. "I'll never find Kay," she said. "Don't worry," replied the reindeer. "The palace is far to the north. I can travel very fast through snow and ice, so I will take you there."

Gerda climbed onto the reindeer's warm and furry back, then they galloped far to the north. At first, there were thick forests on the hills around them but soon, the grass disappeared and the trees died away. After a while, they were surrounded by snow and ice.

Gerda and the reindeer travelled for countless days, until it was so cold that Gerda could barely move. Ahead of them, the night sky was filled with the shimmering, glowing rainbow bands of the northern lights, that lit the reindeer's way.

Finally, Gerda and the reindeer reached the North Pole. They found a great palace that looked as if it had been carved from a single block of ice.

"This must be the ice palace," said Gerda.

As Gerda approached there was a strange, low, rumbling noise. The sound grew louder and then, suddenly, ice creatures, shaped like great bears, rose up from the snow and stood guard at the entrance to the palace. Gerda was afraid, but she found that her hot breath melted the creatures and she passed safely through the entrance to the palace.

Inside, the ice palace was vast and silent. Gerda marvelled at the huge, freezing halls, whose ceilings seemed to stretch upwards to the sky. She shivered in the cold. "I must find Kay," whispered Gerda and she continued to search the Snow Queen's palace.

There were giant, empty halls everywhere. Gerda walked through them and found Kay sitting by the lake, moving pieces of ice around in a daze.

Gerda ran to Kay. She hugged him, but he didn't even notice her. He was too busy trying to solve the impossible puzzle the Snow Queen had set him. Gerda began to cry and her tears touched Kay's face. The warm tears melted all the ice around Kay's heart. He sat up and looked around, as if waking from a dream. "Oh Gerda!" he said, "I'm so glad you're here."

The two friends ran from the frozen palace. Its vast halls echoed with their footsteps. Outside, they climbed onto the reindeer's back and galloped off, before the Snow Queen could return.

It was a long and tiring journey. After many days, the weary friends arrived home, to find that it was summer and the flowers were in bloom. Kay and Gerda played together in the garden, just as they used to do and never again did the Snow Queen freeze Kay's heart.

The Princess and the Pea

Once, there lived a prince who wanted to marry. He travelled all around the world and met many princesses, but he didn't fall in love with any of them. Some were too proud and haughty, while others were rude, or thoughtless. "Finding a wife is so hard," the prince sighed. "If only I could meet a princess who was kind and sensitive."

After his travels, the prince returned to his home town, where his parents, the king and queen, greeted him. "Don't worry," the queen said, "I'm sure you'll meet the right princess, one day."

That night, there was a terrible storm. Thunder crashed and lightning flashed. Inside the palace, the king and queen were just about to go to bed when there was a knock at the door. The king opened it to find a pretty young woman standing on the doorstep. She was soaked to the skin.

The queen sat the young woman in front of the fire to dry her clothes. "Why have you come here, my dear?" she asked.
"I am a poor servant girl, looking for work," replied the young woman. "Please don't turn me away."

The prince had heard the knocking and came to see who it was. When he saw the girl, he fell instantly in love with her. The prince sat and talked with the young woman for a long time. "I wish she were a princess," he thought. "I would marry her straight away."

Soon, they were laughing together like old friends. "I was raised by a poor couple," the young woman explained. "They always told me that my real parents were royal, but I never believed them. Now that my foster parents have both died, there is no way to find out," she finished, sadly.

That night, the queen had a bed prepared with many mattresses, piled high, on top of each other. "This girl looks like a princess and she acts like a princess," thought the queen. "She must have royal blood and I think I know how to find out." She placed a single pea under the bottom mattress and sent a servant to fetch the young woman.

The queen showed the young woman into the bedroom and put a ladder against the side of the mattresses. "You can sleep here tonight," she said. The young woman thought it was a very strange way to spend the night. However, she was too polite to complain and climbed up the ladder.

The young women lay down on the mattresses and tried to go to sleep, but it was no good. No matter how she tossed and turned, she could feel something under the mattresses. It kept her awake the whole night. When the sun shone through the windows in the morning, she still felt tired. She climbed down the ladder and went out into the hall.

"Did you have a good night's sleep?" asked the queen.

"No," said the young woman, shyly. "I think there was something under the mattresses, it felt like a hard lump. I was tossing and turning all night." At these words, the queen nodded and smiled to herself.

That afternoon, the queen went for a walk with the prince. "I am in love with the servant girl, mother," he said. "I just wish that she was a princess, instead of a servant girl." The prince looked very sad.

The queen smiled at her son. "Don't worry," she said. "The girl really is a true princess. Only someone with royal blood could be delicate enough to feel a single pea under that many mattresses."

The prince was overjoyed at this happy news. He rushed back into the palace to find the princess. As soon as he saw her, he got down on one knee and asked for her hand in marriage. She accepted gladly, for she had fallen in love with the prince when she first set eyes on him.

The prince and the princess were married in the castle and everyone had a great celebration. The princess never did find out why she had to sleep on so many mattresses, but she and the prince lived happily ever after anyway.

The Fox Prince

Once upon a time, a princess named Arabella lived in a palace with her mother and father, the king and queen. The kingdom they ruled was very small and poor. Although the palace was made of marble and had many large rooms, the king and queen could not afford to keep many servants.

One day, a strange man came to the palace. He wore a wide hat with a yellow feather in it and a long, green cloak that reached down to his feet. He had a group of nine red-haired men with him. They also wore big cloaks and wide hats, so that nobody could see their faces clearly. They came into the palace and smiled at everyone. "I am Prince Reynard," said the man, bowing to the king and queen. "I bring you good news. Great riches will come to you."

The king was suspicious. "He doesn't look much like a prince to me," he whispered to the queen.
"Oh, but I assure you I am," said Prince Reynard, who must have had very good hearing. "I travelled to see you because I heard a legend about your palace. It is said that a great treasure is buried deep in the cellars of this castle. To reveal the treasure, everyone in the palace must gather in the cellar. Then, as if by magic, the treasure will appear."

The queen was very excited. "We are in great need of money," she said. "What harm can it do to try this?"
"It sounds very silly to me," said the king, "but if it brings us treasure, who am I to complain?"

So the king ordered everyone in the palace to gather in the Throne Room, ready to find the treasure.

As the king, the queen and the servants walked down to the cellar, Princess Arabella saw that Prince Reynard was hiding something beneath his cloak. It was big and bushy and had a white tip. "That looks just like a fox's tail," thought Princess Arabella! "Look, Mother," she said to the queen. "Prince Reynard has… "
"Not now, dear," interrupted the queen. "We're far too busy."

Arabella didn't want to go into the cellar. She ran and hid behind a curtain and watched as everyone else climbed down the steps. She noticed that Prince Reynard and his men stayed at the rear.

When the last person had gone into the cellar, Prince Reynard looked around quickly, gave a sly chuckle and promptly slammed the cellar door shut.
He turned the key in the lock, so that the people of the palace could not get out.
Prince Reynard jumped in the air and clicked his heels together. "Hooray!" he said. "My cunning plan has worked, my fox brothers, the palace is now ours."

Suddenly, Arabella realised that Prince Reynard wasn't a man at all.
He was really a big, red fox, standing on his hind legs. His nine men threw off their cloaks and they were foxes, too. "Three cheers for the Fox Prince!" cried the other foxes and they carried the Fox Prince to the Throne Room.

Arabella tiptoed over to the cellar door, but the Fox Prince had taken the key. She spoke to the king through the keyhole. "Help!" called the king from inside the cellar. "There's no treasure! We're trapped! You must get the key, Arabella. Then we can chase the foxes away. But it won't be so easy to fool them, they are cunning beasts."

The foxes were all over the palace. They left muddy pawprints on the beds. They went into the kitchen and carried off the tastiest food. They opened the henhouses and chased the chickens. They frightened the horses in the stables and swung on the chandeliers.

Prince Reynard lounged on the throne, with the king's best crown on his head, while his fox servants brought him the daintiest dishes from the kitchens.

In the meantime, Arabella had thought of a plan. She walked into the throne room, where the foxes were dancing and drinking the palace's finest wine. "Hello, great Prince," said Arabella.

"Seize her!" cried the Fox Prince. "Put her in the cellar with the others."

"Wait," said Arabella. "I have a puzzle for you. But I don't think you're clever enough to solve it."

The Fox Prince was suddenly interested. He held up a paw to stop the other foxes grabbing the princess. He was a very proud fox and didn't like being told he wasn't clever. "I can solve any puzzle," he said. "Tell me what it is, princess."

Princess Arabella took a big, deep breath and told the foxes her puzzle. "In this palace are ten fine brushes that would clean up the mess you have made," she said. "But no matter where you look, they will always be behind you. If you can find them, I'll go into the cellar. If you can't, you have to let everyone out."

The foxes searched the palace, sniffing in every corner. But they couldn't find the brushes. "You're a liar," said the Fox Prince, after he returned to the throne room. He was panting from his search. "There are no such brushes." Arabella laughed. "The brushes are your own tails, you silly foxes!"
The Fox Prince felt behind him for his tail and laughed. "You win, princess," he admitted. He held out the cellar key for her.

Arabella took the key from the Fox Prince and ran to the cellar door. She unlocked it and the king and his servants quickly chased all the foxes out of the palace and into the woods. As the Fox Prince left, Arabella thought she heard him cry, "Goodbye, Arabella. It was a pleasure to be outfoxed by you!"

The Fox Prince never returned to the palace and the king, the queen and Arabella, lived happily every after.

Twelve Dancing Princesses

A king once had twelve daughters. They were good daughters, except for one, very strange thing. Every night, the princesses left their shoes by their beds. Every morning, the shoes would be completely worn out. Whenever the king asked the princesses why this was, they giggled and ran off.

The king spent so much money on new shoes for his daughters, that the kingdom began to run out of money. The king decided that something had to be done. He issued a proclamation throughout the land, "Whoever can find out what happens to my daughters' shoes will become heir to the throne. He may also marry any of my daughters. But whoever fails to find out the secret in three days, will be banished."

One brave knight after another vowed to find out the secret of the twelve dancing princesses. They tried to stay up all night, but when the sun came up each one found that he had drifted into a deep sleep. The shoes were worn out and there was no clue as to how it had happened. These knights were banished, just as the king had promised.

One day, a soldier returned to the kingdom after a long time away.
When he heard about the proclamation, he went to the king. "I will find out the
princesses' secret," said the soldier. "I have spent my life fighting. A few princesses
don't scare me."

While the soldier was walking back from the palace to his cottage, he met an
old, wise woman and told her of his quest. "Here," said the wise woman, holding
out her hands. "Take this cloak."

"What cloak?" asked the soldier.

"It is a cloak of invisibility," said the wise woman.

The soldier held the invisible cloak. Even though he couldn't see it, he could feel its soft material in his hands. "Pretend to be asleep when the princesses call you," said the wise woman. "Then, put on the cloak. However, make sure you don't eat, or drink anything they give you."

The next night, after the princesses had got ready for bed, the soldier stood guard over them. "Take this drink," said the eldest princess, handing the soldier a goblet. "It will warm you through the night." The soldier pretended to drink from the goblet, but he secretly poured it away and pretended to fall fast asleep.

The princesses sat up in bed and looked at the soldier. "Quick," said the eldest princess. "Let's go!" She opened a trap door in the floor and the princesses put on their shoes and went through it. Quickly slipping on the cloak of invisibility, the soldier followed them.

The princesses walked down a stairway into a dark tunnel. The soldier followed too closely and stepped on the youngest princess' dress.

"Someone stepped on my dress!" she said, fearfully.

"Nonsense," said the eldest princess. "Hurry up, the princes are waiting."

The tunnel opened out into a wonderful land, filled with shining trees. As they passed through, the soldier saw that the leaves on the trees were made of silver. The soldier broke off a silver twig and the youngest princess heard the sound. "There is someone here," she said again, but the others told her not to be so silly.

Next, the princesses passed through a land where the trees had leaves made of gold. Then they visited a third land, where the trees had leaves of solid diamonds. The soldier had to shade his eyes, because the trees were so dazzling.

The princesses arrived at a wide, underground lake. There, twelve fairy princes, wearing glittering clothes, waited in twelve little boats. They rowed the princesses across the great lake. The soldier hid in the youngest princess' boat. No one noticed him because the magic cloak made him invisible.

When they reached the far shore, the soldier saw that they had travelled to Fairyland. Music started up from unseen instruments and the princes and the princesses danced all night. When they were tired, they drank from golden goblets.

At last, it was time to return. The soldier made sure he got back to the bedroom first. When the princesses arrived, the soldier pretended to be snoring. "It's a shame that this soldier must be banished when he fails to find out our secret," said the eldest, "but we have been bewitched and there is nothing we can do."

The next night, the soldier followed the princesses again. This time, he took a twig from one of the golden trees. On the third and last night, the soldier followed them and took a twig from a diamond tree. While the princesses danced, the soldier took a goblet and brought it back with him. The next day, the soldier came to the king. "Tell me the princesses' secret," the king said, "or I will banish you like the rest."

"The princesses have been bewitched by twelve fairy princes," said the soldier. When he showed the king and the princesses the twigs and the goblet, the spell on the princesses was broken. The king was no longer angry and hugged his daughters to him. "You may choose any of my daughters to marry," he said to the soldier.

The soldier thought for a long time. "The eldest is my choice," he said. "She is the cleverest of them all." The eldest princess married the soldier gladly and they lived happily ever after.

The Princess' Song

A long time ago, in a faraway land, there lived a good and wise queen who loved to sing. But then her kingdom was conquered by an evil king and the queen was cast out of her castle. The queen had a baby daughter, called Melody. She knew that Melody would be in danger if the evil king found her, so the queen gave the baby to a poor farmer and his wife. "Keep her safe from the king," said the queen.

A passing fortune teller saw the queen saying goodbye to her baby. "One day, this child will rule the land," said the fortune teller. The queen felt very sad. She said goodbye to her baby and sang a song, "Worry not, in days to come. The princess will return to claim her own."

The farmer and his wife already had two little boys, but they took care of the queen's child and brought her up as their own. Years passed and Melody grew to be a kind and beautiful girl.

Melody's step-brothers grew to be strong boys, but they were jealous of her because she was a princess. The brothers called her names and made her clean the pig sty and work in the fields. However, Melody always stayed cheerful and would often sing to herself. She had a voice even purer and more lovely than her mother, the queen.

In time, the evil king died and his son ruled the kingdom. The new king was much kinder and nobler than his father. He loved singing and dancing. Wandering minstrels and acrobats were always welcome at the castle.

One day, the king decided to hold a contest to find the best singers and dancers in the land. His messengers went to tell the people of the kingdom. "The winners will each get a medal of solid gold!" they shouted.

The farmer and his wife thought that Melody had the most beautiful voice they had ever heard. They insisted that she enter the contest, so Melody began to practice her singing.

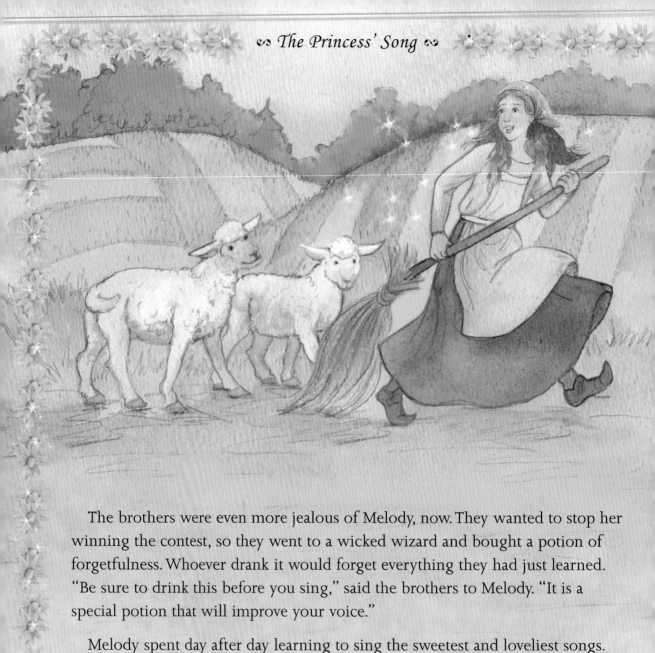

The brothers were even more jealous of Melody, now. They wanted to stop her winning the contest, so they went to a wicked wizard and bought a potion of forgetfulness. Whoever drank it would forget everything they had just learned. "Be sure to drink this before you sing," said the brothers to Melody. "It is a special potion that will improve your voice."

Melody spent day after day learning to sing the sweetest and loveliest songs. She sang while she dug in the fields and while she tended the sheep on the farm.

At last, the day of the contest came. There were singers, dancers, acrobats and storytellers. There was even a circus, with fire-eaters, jugglers and horse-riders. They had all come to win the prizes.

The young king lounged on his throne, looking bored. One by one, the minstrels and puppeteers stood in front of him and performed. The king didn't even smile when he saw them. "This is extremely dull," he said. "I have seen all these people before. I wish there were one who was different!"

Finally, it was Melody's turn to perform in front of the king. She uncorked the potion that the brothers had given her and drank it in one go. Then she stepped out in front of the throne. She was so nervous that her hands were shaking.

"Sing," said the king, hardly bothering to look at her.

Melody took a deep breath and found that she had forgotten every single one of the songs she had learned. She stood there, fearful and wide-eyed. Then she remembered one song. It was the one the queen had sung to her when she was a baby. She sang, "Worry not, in days to come. The princess will return to claim her own."

Everyone in the castle stopped to listen. They had never heard such a beautiful sound. When the king heard the words of Melody's song, he knew that she must be the lost princess. He jumped from his throne and knelt on one knee in front of her. "Marry me," he said, "and we can rule the kingdom together."

Melody married the king and there was great rejoicing throughout the kingdom. They lived happily ever after till the end of their days and the castle was always filled with joyful song.